About Starters Stories

This new range of books offers a stimulating selection of fiction for young readers to tackle themselves. The language is graded into three reading levels — red, blue, and green. The stories are accompanied by colorful and lively illustrations.

The topic dealt with in each STORY is expanded upon in an accompanying STARTERS FACTS book, which provides a valuable source of information and topic-based activities.

In this case the fantasy **Anna and the Moon Queen** is matched by an informative FACTS book called **Moon.**

Reading Consultants

Betty Root, Tutor-in-charge, Center for the Teaching of Reading, University of Reading.

Geoffrey Ivimey, Senior Lecturer in Child Development, University of London Institute of Education.

Anna and the Moon Queen

by
Jenny Vaughan

illustrated by
Barbara Bailey

Starters Stories · Green 2

Once, long ago and far away deep in the mountains, there was a small country. The king there was wicked and cruel, and he made his people work day and night, mining for silver in the mountains.

The people had no time to look after their own farms and houses. Everything was in ruins. Every day donkeys carried cartloads of silver to the palace. But still the king wanted more.

The palace servants were the only
people who did not work in the
mine. There were only a few of
them. Most were too young, too sick,
or too weak to dig for silver. Anna
was one of the servants.

Anna was small and thin. No one
noticed her, but she noticed
everyone. She noticed the unhappy
people, and she noticed the king.
He wandered around on the roof
night after night, watching the moon.

The king thought that the moon was
made of silver, and he wanted it for
himself. He made the people build a
tall tower on top of a high mountain.
But the tower was not tall enough to
reach the moon. So the wise men of
the kingdom made a telescope.

They put the telescope on the tower
and the king looked through it. He
saw that the moon was very large,
and he wanted it even more.

The king was the only person allowed
to look through the telescope. But
one night, Anna crept up to the top
of the tower and looked through it.
The moon seemed strange, empty
and dusty. It did not look like silver.

Suddenly the king was upon Anna.
'Why are you looking through my
telescope?' he shouted.
'I was looking to see if the moon
really is made of silver,' said Anna.
'I don't think it is.'

The king grew angrier and angrier.
'You lie!' he said. 'I will punish you for
saying that, and for looking through my
telescope, at my moon.'
He threw Anna into a dungeon and
called his wise men to the palace.

'Make me a machine,' he said, 'to
take someone to the moon. If you
fail, you will be punished.'
The wise men were afraid. They built
a strange machine on top of the
high tower.

On the day the machine was ready
the king went to the dungeons. He
found Anna, and told her she was
going to the moon.
'Bring back a piece of the moon,' he
said. 'If you don't, I will throw you
from the top of the high tower.'

Anna was afraid, but there was
nothing she could do. She sat in the
machine, and closed her eyes.
There was a loud bang, and the
machine soared into space.

Anna looked down at the earth. She could no longer see the kingdom or the mountains. Then the machine began to shake and crack. Pieces fell away. Anna fell through the sky.

Far below, she could see the earth getting bigger and bigger. She could see all the countries beneath her and she thought she was going to die. But then something caught her, and she stopped falling.

She looked up and saw large wings
beating above her. A giant white owl
held her in its claws.
'Don't be afraid,' said the owl. 'I am
the servant of the Queen of the Moon.
I am taking you to her kingdom.'
Soon Anna was on the moon.

She looked around. The owl had
vanished. The light was bright, but
the moon was bare and dusty. The
Queen of the Moon appeared. She
was tall and very beautiful, and wore
a long, shining cloak.

'Welcome to my kingdom,' she said.
'Why have you come? There is
nothing here but dust and rocks.'
'My king sent me,' said Anna. 'He
thinks the moon is made of silver. He
wants it for himself.'

The Queen of the Moon was angry.
She grew tall and frightening.
'The moon is mine!' she said.
'No one must have it but me!'

But the Queen of the Moon felt sorry
for Anna.
'Your king is a fool,' she said softly.
'There is no silver for him here. Take
that small stone by your feet,' she
said, and vanished.

As Anna picked up the stone, the great owl appeared again. He carried her back to earth. Soon she could see the mountains and the kingdom below her. Then she saw the palace. The owl put her down and flew away.

Anna went to look for the king. He
was in the palace counting great
piles of silver.
'So! You are back!' he said. 'What
have you brought me?'
'A piece of the moon,' said Anna.

When the king saw the stone he was
angrier than he had ever been.
'You have cheated me!' he shouted.
'You have found silver, but you want
to keep it. I will throw you off the
high tower.'

Night was falling as Anna went to
the tower. The king took her to the
top. The people stopped working to
watch. They were afraid, but there
was nothing they could do.

24

Suddenly there was the sound of huge wings, beating. The great owl appeared out of the sky, and snatched up the king. The owl carried him off into the night sky, to the dark side of the moon.

The people never saw the king
again. They left the mines, and went
back to their farms. Anna was free
too. She lived happily ever after in
a little house, deep in the mountains.

Each information book is linked to a story in the new **Starters** program. Both kinds of book are graded into progressive reading levels — red, blue, and green. Titles in the program include:

Starters Facts

RED 1: Going to the Zoo
RED 2: Birds
RED 3: Clowns
RED 4: Going to the Hospital
RED 5: Going to School

BLUE 1: Space Travel
BLUE 2: Cars
BLUE 3: Dinosaurs
BLUE 4: Christmas
BLUE 5: Trains

GREEN 1: Airport
GREEN 2: Moon
GREEN 3: Forts and Castles
GREEN 4: Stars
GREEN 5: Earth

Starters Stories

RED 1: Zoo for Sale
RED 2: The Birds from Africa
RED 3: Sultan's Elephants
RED 4: Rosie's Hospital Story
RED 5: Danny's Class

BLUE 1: The Space Monster
BLUE 2: The Red Racing Car
BLUE 3: The Dinosaur's Footprint
BLUE 4: Palace of Snow
BLUE 5: Mountain Express

GREEN 1: Flight into Danger
GREEN 2: Anna and the Moon Queen
GREEN 3: The Secret Castle
GREEN 4: The Lost Starship
GREEN 5: Nuka's Tale

First published 1980 by
Macdonald Educational Ltd.,
Holywell House,
Worship Street,
London EC2

© Macdonald Educational Ltd. 1980

ISBN 0-382-06507-7
Published in the United States by
Silver Burdett Company
Morristown, New Jersey
1980 Printing

Library of Congress
Catalog Card No. 80-52516

Editor: Annabel McLaren
Teacher Panel: Susan Alston, Susan Batten, Ann Merriman, Julia Rickell, Gwen Trier
Production: Rosemary Bishop